The Wolf Cupboard

First published 2012 by A & C Black,
an imprint of Bloomsbury Publishing Plc
50 Bedford Square, London WC1B 3DP

www.acblack.com
www.bloomsbury.com

Copyright © 2012 A & C Black
Text copyright © 2012 Susan Gates
Illustrations copyright © 2012 Cherry Whytock

The rights of Susan Gates and Cherry Whytock to be identified
as the author and illustrator of this work have been asserted by them
in accordance with the Copyrights, Designs and Patents Act 1988.

ISBN 978-1-4081-5502-8

A CIP catalogue for this book is available from the British Library.

This book is produced using paper that is made from wood
grown in managed, sustainable forests. It is natural, renewable
and recyclable. The logging and manufacturing processes conform
to the environmental regulations of the country of origin.

Printed by CPI Group (UK), Croydon, CR0 4YY

1 3 5 7 9 10 8 6 4 2

recommended by

www.catchup.org

Catch Up is a not-for-profit charity
which aims to address the problem of
underachievement that has its roots in
literacy and numeracy difficulties.

The Wolf Cupboard

Susan Gates

A & C Black • London

Contents

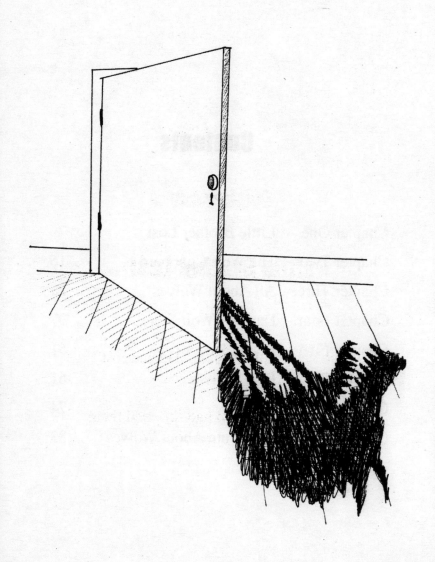

Chapter One

Little Brother Lost

Leon was in big trouble. He had lost
Danny, his little brother.

That morning, Mum had dropped them
both off at school.

She had told Leon: "This is Danny's first
day at school. Make sure he knows where the
toilets are. Make sure no big kids bully him."

And Leon had said, "Don't worry, Mum.
He'll be all right with me."

Leon had meant to check on Danny at morning break. But he forgot. He played football with his friends instead.

When the bell rang for home time, Leon went running out of the school gates. Then he suddenly remembered. He was supposed to be walking Danny home!

He ran back to find Danny.

The babies' class had already come out of school. Mums, dads and carers were taking them home.

Leon looked around for his little brother's cheeky grin.

But there was no sign of Danny anywhere.

"Mum will kill me if anything happens to him!" thought Leon.

Everyone went home. The playground was empty and quiet. And still no Danny.

Then Leon really started to panic.

"Where are you, Danny?" he whispered, his voice shaky.

He felt sick. What if Danny had gone home without him? There was a busy road between school and home. Danny was only four years old. Leon had scary pictures in his mind, of Danny getting run over.

Or what if some bad person took him away?

Leon couldn't even *think* about that. He blocked it out of his mind.

Then he heard a noise. A kind of whimper, coming from behind the school bins.

Leon ran over. "Danny? Danny? Is that you?"

Leon shoved the big, heavy bin out of the way. And there was Danny, hiding behind it.

Leon was really pleased to see his little
brother. But he was angry too because he had
been so scared that Danny was lost.

"Danny!" he yelled. "I nearly had a heart attack! I thought you'd gone home without me!"

Danny looked up. His face was covered with snot and tears. He looked really scared.

"What's the matter, Danny?" asked Leon. "Has someone hurt you?"

Chapter Two

The Wolf Cupboard

Danny gave a big sniff and wiped the snot from his nose with his sleeve.

"Hurry up and tell me!" said Leon.

"This big boy..." Danny began.

"What!" yelled Leon. "Did a big boy hurt you? Tell me his name!"

"I don't know his name," said Danny. "He was just some big boy."

"Did he hurt you?" asked Leon again.

"No," said Danny. "He told me about the wolf cupboard."

"The what?" said Leon. "What wolf cupboard?"

Danny began to cry again. "That big boy told me if you're bad at school they shut you up in the wolf cupboard. And there's a big, bad wolf in there. And he eats you all up."

Leon felt his fear rush away, like water down a plug hole. He burst out laughing.

"Danny!" he grinned. "There's no such thing as a wolf cupboard!"

"Yes there is a wolf cupboard!" said
Danny, still crying. "That big boy showed it
to me. It's outside my classroom."

"He was just trying to scare you," said Leon. "Look, Danny, wolves don't live in cupboards."

But Danny wasn't listening. He gave a big shiver.

"I hate this school," he told Leon. "And I'm never, ever coming back here again!"

"Oh no!" thought Leon.

He'd promised to look after Danny. But
what would Mum say if he took Danny home
crying and scared and saying he was never,
ever going to school again?

"Mum will kill me!" thought Leon.

She was on early shifts at work. So
Leon would have to walk Danny to school
tomorrow.

"What if he won't go?" thought Leon.
"What if I have to drag him crying and
screaming down the High Street?"

Things were looking really bad.

"I'll just have to show Danny that this wolf cupboard is a load of rubbish!" thought Leon.

He grabbed Danny's hand. "Come on," he said. "Show me where this wolf cupboard is."

"No!" yelled Danny. "I'm not going near it!"

"Calm down," said Leon. "We won't go anywhere near it. I want you to show it to me. Just *show* me. All right?"

Leon dragged Danny back into school.

It was ages since Leon had been in the
infant school. It felt really strange. The
chairs and tables seemed tiny.

Danny pointed a shaking finger. "There it
is!"

Leon said, "What, that little cupboard?"

He almost laughed again. But he stopped himself because Danny looked so scared.

"That cupboard must look really huge to a four-year-old," Leon thought.

Leon went up to the cupboard.

"Don't open it!" yelled Danny. "Don't open it! Please!"

Leon wanted to open the cupboard to show Danny there was nothing to be scared of. But the cupboard was locked shut.

"See?" said Danny. "That's so the wolf can't get out!"

"But there *isn't* any wolf!" said Leon.

"Yes, there is!" shouted Danny. "Me and this big boy, we saw my teacher going up to the cupboard with a big stick. And the big boy said she was going to check on the wolf and if she didn't bash it with the stick, it would eat her too!"

Leon gave a big sigh. "Did you see the teacher open the cupboard? Did you see her bash the wolf?"

"I saw her open the cupboard," said Danny. "But then I ran away in case the wolf jumped out and gobbled me up. And I hid behind the bin."

Leon gave an even bigger sigh. It was going to be hard work, making Danny see that this wolf didn't exist.

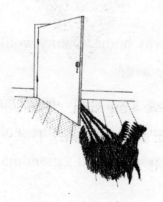

Chapter Three

All About Wolves

On the way home, Danny wouldn't shut up about the wolf.

"It's a big, grey wolf," said Danny. "With great big sharp teeth. Like the wolf that ate Little Red Riding Hood's grandma."

"Did the big kid tell you that rubbish?" asked Leon.

"No, I thought of that all by myself," said Danny.

As they walked past the library, Leon suddenly remembered, "I have to take Mum's book back."

He got the book out of his backpack. He was just handing it in at the counter when he heard Danny yell, "This is what that wolf is like!"

"Oh no!" thought Leon.

Danny had found a book about wolves. He was looking at a photo of a huge, grey wolf. It was like the big, bad wolf from fairy tales. Its fierce, yellow eyes stared right at you out of the page.

It had sharp fangs. They looked strong
enough to crunch your bones. They were
dripping blood.

"Look at his teeth!" yelled Danny. "He's just eaten a bad boy!"

"No he hasn't!" said Leon. "And anyway, if he only eats bad boys, why can't you just be good?"

"Because I can't be good all the time!" Danny shouted back. "I'm bound to get put in that wolf cupboard. So I'm not going to school. Not ever again."

Leon almost said a bad word. But then he saw the librarian staring at him. So he said it inside his head.

"Are all little brothers such a pain in the neck?" he thought.

Leon grabbed the book. "This is a stupid book!" he said. He slammed it shut and was about to shove it back on the shelf when he saw the cover.

The book was called *All About Wolves*. There was a lot of stuff written on the front. But some words seemed to leap out at Leon.

"How To Avoid a Wolf Attack," they said.

And suddenly Leon had a brilliant plan. It was so brilliant he was proud of himself.

He had given up trying to tell Danny the wolf didn't exist. But he could use this book to show him that he didn't have to be scared of it.

"And then everything will be all right
again," thought Leon. "And Mum won't kill
me when I get home!"

Leon told Danny, "I'm going to borrow
this book right now!"

"But you said it was a stupid book," said
Danny.

"I've changed my mind," said Leon.
"This is a great book. This book will save my
life!"

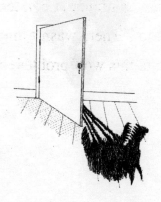

Chapter Four

Danny's Wolf Stare

When they got home, Leon took Danny up to his bedroom. There wasn't much time. He had to sort out this wolf problem before Mum got home.

"Right," said Leon, flicking through the book again to find the page on "How To Avoid a Wolf Attack".

Danny was not in a good mood. His lower lip stuck out like a fat pink slug. He was chanting, "I'm not going back to school. I'm not going back to school!"

"Will you stop saying that?" snapped Leon. "I'm trying to help you. I'm trying to make sure that, even if you *do* get chucked in the wolf cupboard, you won't get eaten. So there's no need to be scared. OK?"

"OK," said Danny. But he didn't sound sure.

Leon found the right page and read it. "These are great tips," he thought. But would they work for Danny?

"Imagine there's this great big angry wolf, with very sharp teeth," said Leon. "And it wants to bite you!"

Leon showed his teeth, like an angry wolf. He gave a loud growl. "Grrrr!"

"You're scaring me!" cried Danny.

"But you don't need to be scared!" said Leon. "Because this book tells you what to do."

"What do I do?" asked Danny.

"Well," said Leon, "you do what another wolf would do. You stare at the wolf."

"What, just stare at it?" said Danny, puzzled.

"Yes!" said Leon. "It's called a wolf stare. The wolf in the photo is doing it. Wolves stare fiercely at each other. And the one with the fiercest stare wins."

"What, like this?" asked Danny making his eyes big and round.

"That's really good," Leon said.

Danny kept staring, his eyes wide, not blinking.

"You can stop staring now," said Leon. "It's creepy!"

Finally, Danny blinked. "But what if the other wolf has a fiercer stare than me?" he asked. "What if it wins? Will it bite me?"

Leon could hear Mum turning her key in the front door. He looked at the book for an answer.

"No, the wolf won't bite you," said Leon. "You've just got to do *this*."

Leon rolled onto his back, like a dog that wants to have its tummy tickled.

"What are you doing?" asked Danny.

Leon said, "The book tells you, if a wolf loses a staring contest, it rolls over onto its back, like this. It's like saying, 'I give in.' And then the other wolf won't bite."

"Oh, I get it!" said Danny. He rolled over onto his back too.

"And if you whimper as well," Leon told him, "the other wolf knows for sure you've given in."

"Like this?" said Danny, whimpering and pawing at the air with his hands.

"That's really great!" said Leon.

Mum looked round the bedroom door.

"What are you two up to?" she said.

"We're pretending to be wolves," said Danny.

Leon went red. He felt really silly rolling around on the floor.

At least only Mum had seen him, and not his mates at school. They would have laughed their socks off.

Mum went back downstairs. Leon stopped pretending to be a wolf. He stood up.

"Now, remember, Danny," he said. "If you get chucked in the wolf cupboard, you can use your wolf stare. And if that doesn't work..."

"I know," said Danny. "I roll on my back and give in."

"Right!" said Leon. "You've got it!"

"I'm not scared of that wolf now," said Danny.

Leon thought, "My plan has worked like a dream!"

But you never knew with little brothers. Who could tell what went on in their heads?

Just then Mum came back into the bedroom. She asked Danny, "Did you like your first day at school?"

"Well, I didn't like school *at first*," began Danny.

Mum frowned. Leon held his breath. He was thinking, "Please Danny, don't make trouble for me!"

Then Danny put a big smile on his face.

"But everything's all right now," he told Mum. "So I'm going again tomorrow."

Mum was smiling too. Leon thought, "Phew! I'm not going to get into trouble!"

But what would happen tomorrow? When Danny woke up, would he still not be scared of the wolf in the cupboard?

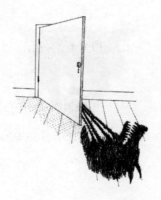

Chapter Five

Really Uncool!

Next morning, Danny seemed quite happy when he got up.

He didn't say, "I'm not going to school!"

Leon thought, "My plan is working really well!"

There was just one tricky moment. When
Mum gave Danny his cornflakes she asked
him, "Why are you staring at me like that?
It's creepy!"

"I'm practising my fierce wolf stare,"
Danny told her, with wide unblinking eyes.

A bit later, when Leon walked Danny to school, they passed a gang of tough-looking teenagers, leaning against a wall.

"Why is that little kid staring at us like that?" one of them asked Leon. "Is he trying to be funny?"

"No, no," Leon told them, dragging Danny away. "He's only four. He doesn't even know what he's doing."

"Yes I do!" yelled Danny. "I'm practising my fierce...!"

"Will you shut up?" hissed Leon, clamping his hand over Danny's mouth. "You'll get me into a fight! Save that stare for the wolf cupboard."

"OK!" agreed Danny. "I'll practise giving up instead."

He rolled onto the pavement, whimpering and waving his paws in the air.

"You do it as well!" he said to Leon.

"Are you crazy?" said Leon. "There are people watching!"

Danny's eyes began to fill with tears. "If you don't help me," he said, "I'm not going to school."

"Oh no!" thought Leon. He checked his watch. They had only ten minutes to get to school!

Leon looked around again. None of his mates was about.

"All right," he told Danny. "I'll pretend to be a wolf. But only for five seconds. Then will you come to school?"

"OK," said Danny.

So Leon threw himself on his back on the pavement. He waved his arms and legs about. He whimpered. He put his tongue out of his mouth like a panting dog.

"Hey, you're a great wolf," said Danny.

There was a bus going past. Leon looked
up.

Some girls he knew were staring at him from the window.

"Oh no!" thought Leon. "They're going to think I'm really uncool!"

He jumped to his feet. He grabbed Danny's hand. He dragged him along the street and into school.

All that day, in lessons, Leon thought about Danny. How was his little brother doing?

"With any luck," thought Leon, "he's forgotten all about the wolf in the cupboard."

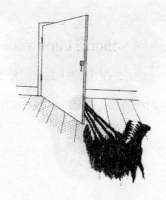

Chapter Six

Real Wolves

At the end of school, Leon waited for the baby class to come out. At last, he saw Danny running towards him, with a big smile on his face.

"Phew!" thought Leon. "He looks OK."

But, as they walked home, Danny asked him, "Will you read me some more of that wolf book?"

"Why?" said Leon. "You'll only get scared again."

"I won't," said Danny. "I told you, I'm not scared of wolves any more."

"No!" said Leon. "No more wolves!"

Wolves were nothing but trouble. They
had nearly got him into a fight with those
teenagers. They had made those girls on the
bus think he was really uncool.

But Danny went on and on until Leon
agreed.

So, that night, Leon sat on Danny's bed
and opened the book *All About Wolves*.

"Just five minutes' reading," said Leon.
"And you've got to promise me you won't get
scared."

"I promise," said Danny.

Leon looked down the page, to find
something nice to say about wolves.

"Hey," he told Danny, "it says here most people are totally wrong about wolves. Real wolves are nothing like the big, bad wolves in fairy tales."

"So what are they like, then?" asked Danny.

"It says real wolves are shy. They run away from people. They only attack you if you hurt them first. Or try to hurt their cubs. I didn't know that," said Leon, getting interested.

He turned over a few pages. "Hey!" he said again. "It says wolves make really good parents. And you know when they howl?"

"Yes," said Danny. "I'm good at howling." He threw back his head and gave a really loud howl.

"Cool!" said Leon. "That's a great howl!"

Mum yelled up the stairs, "What's going on? You and Danny aren't fighting, are you?"

Leon shouted down, "No, Mum!" He turned to the book again.

"When wolves howl," he told Danny, "it's like they're talking to each other. You can hear a howl ten miles away!"

"Wow!" said Danny. "Ten miles!"

Danny opened his mouth and gave a howl so loud it seemed to shake the house.

"No more howling!" said Leon, putting his hands over his ears. "Mum will wonder what's going on."

He flipped over another page in the book.

"The guy that wrote this lived with wolves in Alaska," he told Danny. "He made friends with them. Look at this!"

Leon showed Danny the book.

It was the scary grey wolf from the other photo. And the man who lived with wolves was sitting beside him, scratching his ears, as if he was a great big friendly pet dog.

Suddenly Danny said, his eyes shining, "I could be friends with that wolf in the cupboard!"

Leon slammed the book shut. "Oh no!" he thought. "My plan is going all wrong!"

"That wolf could be my best friend!" said Danny.

"I've played along with this stupid wolf in the cupboard story for far too long," Leon thought. "Now it's time to get tough!"

"Look, Danny," said Leon. "I told you before. There *isn't* any wolf in that cupboard. Only silly little kids would believe that. There *isn't* a wolf who eats bad kids."

"I know there isn't," said Danny.

"At last!" thought Leon. "He's got it!"

But then Danny went on, "I *know* he doesn't eat kids. Because wolves are really nice. That book says so. Poor wolf, I bet he's lonely in that cupboard. I bet he's just waiting for me to be friends with him."

"Danny!" yelled Leon. "Will you listen to me?"

But Danny's eyes were shut. He had a
happy smile on his face.

And Leon knew just what he was thinking.
Danny was thinking about walking down
the street, with a big, wild wolf by his side.
While the other kids stared and pointed and
said, "Wow! How cool is that?"

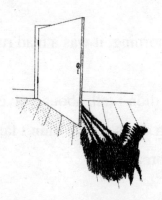

Chapter Seven

Bad Boy

Next morning, it was a mad rush to get to school.

Danny didn't talk about wolves while he was getting dressed. He didn't talk about wolves at breakfast.

"Maybe he's finally got bored with wolves," thought Leon.

Today Mum was dropping them off. As she stood by the car, yelling "Hurry up!", Leon rushed back upstairs to get *All About Wolves*.

"I don't need this book any more," he thought. "I'll take it back to the library on the way home."

At school, Leon was trying to do some tricky sums when the classroom door burst open. A kid from the baby class came running in.

"Miss says Leon's got to come *right away!*" he yelled, as if they were all deaf. "It's about Danny!"

"What's wrong now?" thought Leon.

When Leon got to the baby class, Danny's teacher looked puzzled.

"I don't get it," she told Leon. "For two days Danny has been as good as gold. But today he's been really naughty. He's been running around the classroom, yelling and throwing books on the floor."

Leon looked around the room. He saw Danny sitting at the back with his lip stuck out like a big pink slug and a frown on his face.

"It's almost like he *wants* to be punished," said the teacher. "Do you know what's going on?"

"I think I do," said Leon. "Can I talk to Danny outside?"

"Of course," said Danny's teacher.

Leon marched to the back of the class.

"Come with me!" he hissed at Danny. "I know what you're up to."

He took Danny outside the classroom.

"I know your game!" said Leon. "You're trying to get put in that wolf cupboard, aren't you?"

"This silly school!" Danny frowned. "What do I have to do to get put in the wolf cupboard? I've been really bad!"

"This is stupid!" said Leon. "This wolf thing has gone far enough!"

"But I want to meet the wolf!" wailed Danny. "It's cruel, locking him up in there. I want to take him home! I want him and me to be friends!"

"Look, Danny...!" snapped Leon.

But Danny wasn't listening. He was gazing up the corridor, towards the wolf cupboard. "Hey!" he said, smiling. "The wolf cupboard is open!"

Danny ran to the cupboard. Leon raced after him. But Danny was already tugging the door wider.

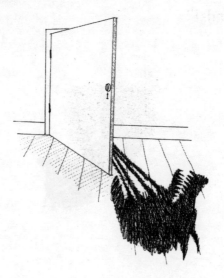

Leon felt a tiny trembling deep in his stomach, as if a wolf with yellow eyes and teeth dripping blood might really leap out.

He skidded to a stop beside Danny. The cupboard door was wide open. It was full of PE stuff, like hoops and footballs and cricket bats. There was hardly room for a mouse in there. Let alone a wolf.

Chapter Eight

The Truth About Wolves

Danny stood, staring into the cupboard.
He didn't speak.

Leon said, "There's no wolf, Danny. Just
like I told you. That stick you saw your
teacher with? I bet it was a cricket bat and she
was just putting it away."

Still Danny didn't speak.

"Danny?" said Leon, more gently, putting a hand on his little brother's shoulder. "You OK?"

Danny burst into tears. He pulled away from Leon and threw himself on the floor. He was crying as if his heart would break.

"I *wanted* there to be a wolf in the cupboard," he wailed. "Where's my wolf?"

Leon didn't know what to do. All he could say was, "*Shhh!* Miss will hear you."

"I've got nothing to take to Show and Tell!" roared Danny.

"What?" said Leon, puzzled.

Then he remembered. When he was in the baby class, kids would bring things in, show them to the other children and talk about them.

"It's Show and Tell this morning," Danny sobbed, "and I was going to take my wolf into my class and tell them all about him."

Suddenly, Leon had another brilliant plan.

"I can't believe it!" he said, pretending to be shocked. "You weren't going to take a wild wolf into the baby class, were you?"

"Why not?" asked Danny. "The book says they hardly ever attack kids."

"I know that," said Leon. "And you know that. But *other* kids don't know that, do they? They only know about the big, bad wolves in fairy tales. If you took a wolf in, they'd say, 'It's going to gobble me all up!' They'd run all over the place, screaming!"

Danny nodded slowly. "I suppose they would be scared," he said.

"Of course they would," said Leon. "I mean, even you were scared at first. Until you learned what wolves are really like. So you've got to tell them the truth in Show and Tell."

Danny wiped away his tears. There was a big smile on his face again.

"That's a good idea!" he said. "I will! I'll tell them the truth!"

Danny got as far as the classroom door. But then he turned round to look at Leon. He'd stopped smiling. His face was like a sad clown.

"But I've got nothing to show!" he wailed. "How can I do Show and Tell when I've got nothing to show!"

"Oh no!" thought Leon.

He'd thought everything was going so well. Now it was all going wrong again!

"Stay here!" he told Danny.

Leon raced back to his classroom and crashed through the door. He tugged *All About Wolves* out of his backpack.

"Back in a minute," he gasped to his teacher then raced off again down the corridor.

He shoved the book into Danny's hand. "Show them this book," he panted. "Show them the photos."

"It's not as good as a real wolf..." Danny began to say.

"But you can't take a real wolf into the classroom!" yelled Leon. "I just told you!"

"Oh yeah," said Danny. "I forgot." And, grasping his book, he trotted back into the baby class.

Leon stood, staring after him. Then he stumbled back to his own classroom.

He felt worn out. He'd worked so hard, sorting out Danny's problems. He should get some kind of medal. But no-one but him would ever know about it.

He slumped back into his seat. At least now he might get some peace.

Minutes ticked by. Then someone in
Leon's class said, "What's that noise?"

Everyone looked up. From the baby class down the corridor came a wild, spine-chilling howl. It made your blood run cold. You could hear it all around the school.

"What on earth was that?" asked Leon's teacher.

Only Leon knew the answer.

It was Danny, doing Show and Tell, teaching his class the truth about wolves.

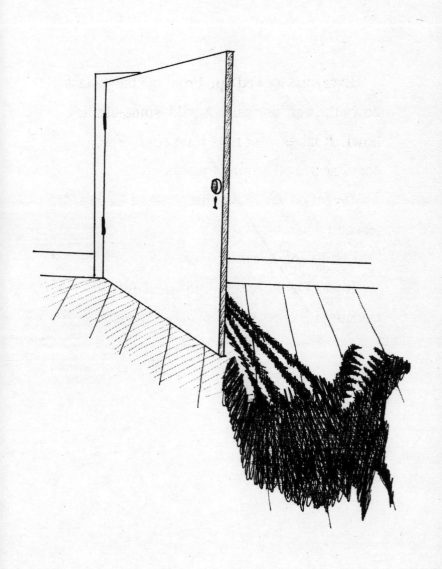